THE LAST

LUDDITE

J. LEE PORTER

&

ED TEJA

ISBN: 978-1-949063-19-6

THE LAST LUDDITE

Irene held up her phone. "Text me," she said.

Lyle Conwell stared at the cell phone and felt his heart sink. "I can't," he said.

"You can't?" she asked. "Just send the address of the restaurant and I'll meet you there."

Irene was a lovely girl and he'd found her fun to talk with. Well-read and lovely were such a perfect combination and now, inevitably, she'd dump him.

He was sure she'd started to like him. They had met at an evening French class at the local library. He'd been drawn to her immediately, but it took him two agonizing weeks to work up the nerve to ask her out. She was willing, but now —

Lyle was shy but technology had made dating even more difficult. Even when he got past the social issues, he faced what seemed to be insurmountable technical complications.

"I can't text anyone anything," he said.

"Why not?" He could see her trying to imagine how that could be.

"I don't have a cell phone."

She stared at him in disbelief for a time. Then her face grew hard. "What do you mean? Did it get stolen?"

"No." Here it came. "I've never had one."

The look on her face told him this was a serious failing in her mind. "You are a Luddite," she said.

"What do you mean?"

She laughed. Was it pity? "I read about them. The people who resisted the Industrial Revolution. They hated technology, modernization. The leader was Ned Ludd. He led riots and his people wrecked machinery because it eliminated jobs. They called themselves Luddites."

"Oh." That rang a bell somewhere. "I just don't care to be leashed to a phone."

"Leashed?" She paused. "Do you have a computer?"

"No."

"An iPod?"

"I don't know what that is."

"Why are you so antisocial?"

His stock was crashing in her eyes. That seemed clear. "I'm not antisocial. I just don't like gadgets. They complicate things."

"They make life so much easier," she said forcefully, letting him know she thought this was important.

"I feel uncomfortable around them. They demand attention."

She shrugged. Everything demands attention. Then her eyes twinkled. "I bet you forgot it at home is all. I've done that. You don't want people to know you forgot it and you used it to tease me."

"I'm not trying to tease," he said.

"I can't go out until next week anyway. Bring your phone to the next class."

She didn't believe him. At least he could hope he could convince her.

Lyle tried to be honest with people about who and what he was. Long before cell phones (he was in his early fifties) he'd been left cold by networking — the old, rubbing-elbows-at-parties style.

Attempting the same thing, interacting over a gadget wasn't his idea of fun. He didn't find it interesting. But then, Lyle Conwell didn't see the advantage in many of the things other people took for granted, the things they loved. In fact, he actively disliked many of them. Most of the time, he was clever enough not to say that out loud.

Maybe he was something of a Luddite.

Whatever it was, people got the wrong idea about him. He wasn't antisocial at all, but unsettled by the unseen world behind electronic communications.

He didn't mind machinery (unlike Ned Ludd). He could understand a physical machine, see it working. Engines made sounds and there was action and reaction; movement and response; if it hangs up here, you bang on it there. If it stops, you take it apart and see what jammed it up.

Technology, electronic devices were different. You could take something apart, but that look inside provided no clues as to how it worked. Nothing you could see moved. Some lights blinked but the physical process, the great what was happening went along invisibly.

And the implications of using them, depending on them, swept you into that unseen current — a current controlled by people you never met.

From the outside, from Lyle's perspective, phones were easily the worst device on the face of the planet. Once everyone began totting them around you couldn't have a discussion with someone without, at some point, the other person deciding you were wrong about something and that it was important, critical even, for them to look it up right then and prove you wrong.

Lyle felt confident that all that multitasking people boasted about was the problem — it was driving people over the brink. The rise in violent crime, mass shootings, and generally absurd behavior were a result of people seeing the world by staring at a device in their hand and not looking around.

That made him a nearly dysfunctional minority.

Even though Lyle wanted no part of it, every day something or someone else tried to convince you to do another thing on a phone. You could bank online, which seemed insane. He liked walking into the bank and talking to people. He relished watching as money changed hands and a real person gave him a receipt that he took home.

Every six months, his car insurance company sent him a letter telling him he could download his current insurance card on his phone. Every six months, he dutifully wrote them a letter telling them: "No, I cannot. I do not have a cell phone. I need a physical card. Please make a note of this."

Even his doctor was put out at his failure to embrace the brave new world.

"Your blood pressure is a bit high," his doctor told him.

Lyle watched the doctor stare at charts and rows of numbers on a tablet computer, examining data and ignoring him.

"What does that mean, that it is high?" Lyle asked, his patience finally worn through like the soles of the old shoes he wore for gardening.

"It should be lower."

Stating the obvious. "Then?"

"We need to monitor it."

Naturally, 'we' meant 'Lyle.'

"Monitor it?"

"This could be just a temporary thing. I hope so. It would help if you ate less salt."

"I can do that."

"But I'd like you to track it."

"The amount of salt I eat?" He pictured himself weighing out an allotment of salt for the day. But what about the salt already in food?"

"No, your blood pressure."

Lyle pointed to the cuff. "I need to get one of those?"

The doctor smiled. "No. It's so much easier than that. Just get yourself one of the new fitness trackers."

"I don't think so."

"They are great. A good one is less than a hundred bucks and will monitor your blood pressure, heart rate, and other factors. It syncs to your cell phone and will automatically send it to me." He tapped on a large monitor. "Our office computer will crunch the data in real time. That will give me a handle on what's causing the problem."

"I don't think so," he said again. "I'd need a cell phone as well, apparently." Forget that he didn't want anyone recording him in real time, even if it was just his blood pressure.

"You don't have a cell phone?"

He shook his head, used to the dismay his admission produced. The shocked look on the doctor's face was appropriate considering the doctor had to think that his obstinate stance single-handedly set back modern medicine by decades.

They worked out a compromise. The doctor insisted he get both items; Lyle agreed to find a healer somewhere who didn't need the tech to do their job.

Arriving at the machine shop where he worked, he found his boss waiting impatiently.

"Morning, Gloria," he said.

She gave him an angry glare. "You are late," she said.

"I told you two days ago that I'd be in late. I had a doctor's appointment this morning."

Her face showed that she remembered now. "I told you to text me the information," she said. "If it isn't in my phone calendar, I can't be expected to remember. And you've screwed up the schedule for the day.

It wasn't the first time that his lack of a cell phone had collided with her inability to function without one.

Fortunately, he was good at his job, which was running machines in a machine shop. If he hadn't been the best machinist his boss had ever worked with (her words), she would have fired him (also her words).

In addition to work, insurance, and medical care, friendships had become complicated. His refusal to have a phone made friends a diminishing commodity.

Unable to text him to have him join them for some event, and unwilling to call his landline and talk, they increasingly just forgot about him.

At some point, Lyle Conwell knew, he had become a dinosaur. His opinion of the world was shared by such a small portion of the population that he couldn't think of anyone else who agreed with it.

His lack of a phone annoyed people. Each thought it was about them. It offended them that they couldn't put his information in their contact list.

His boss, his former friends, all wanted to be able to get ahold of him. Never mind that Lyle didn't want anyone "getting ahold" of him. Partly, he wasn't entirely sure what that meant.

In his world, things were seldom urgent. Messages would keep for a time. They always had. But he lived, increasingly, in a world where no one was watching where they were going, had no idea where they'd been and had the selfies to prove it. This mindset, when he was feeling charitable, struck him as pointless.

Lyle's favorite day was Friday. Friday was usually a good day, and it was payday. After work, he would go to the bank and deposit his check, keeping back a little cash, so that he could stop at the store on the way home.

The small local bank was right on his way home. These days it was easy to find a parking spot and he could always count on a cheerful greeting from Becky, the head teller. There were usually a few people in the bank, taking care of financial business. He seldom saw anyone depositing a check.

Every Friday, when he handed her his endorsed check and the deposit slip, Becky cheerfully reminded him that: "You don't really need to come in every week, Mister Cornwall. You can get cash from an ATM machine."

Picturing the machines he'd seen but never used, imaging them spitting out money, made him cringe.

"But then I wouldn't get to see your smile," he said. Then he held up the receipt. "And I rather like these. Besides, making the trip, coming in somehow makes life more tangible."

"Does it?"

"That's my perception."

"From a banking standpoint, it works the same, regardless of how you do it."

"Does it?"

"Yes. Your employer can deposit your pay directly into your account. You take out cash when and where you need it. Not that you need any these days." Her beaming face told him how wonderful she thought that was.

"The truth is that I like ritual." He rubbed the bills she'd given him together. "I like the feel of money. Most of all I like getting out and seeing people. If I did everything online, I'd have no reason to come into the bank at all."

Her smile persisted, although there was doubt in her eyes. Of course, for her, coming into the bank was work, while Lyle found it a pleasure. He didn't say that. That would be too much for the young woman to process and it might unnerve her completely. She already found him odd, he was certain.

Leaving the bank, he headed for the grocery store, where he found a smiling young woman standing at a card table promoting home deliveries. As people wandered by her, she eagerly extolled the virtues of having the store shop for you.

"You give us an idea of the kinds of meals you eat, and every week we will deliver all the ingredients for those and even recipes you might like to try. Based on your online feedback, we will tweak the meals, adapt them over time. As we learn what appeals to you, we can suggest things based on fruits and vegetables that are in season, even supply recipes that will let you prepare delicious meals right at home."

She had the enthusiasm of a true believer (almost everything had true believers) but his cynical nature wondered if it was actually enthusiasm that came from anticipating a healthy commission from sales.

Of course, there was no reason at all it couldn't be some serendipitous combinations of the two. No reason at all.

And there was nothing wrong with it either.

At the French class that night (it was a Monday and Friday class), he tried to get Irene to agree to meet him at a restaurant that he knew. "It's French," he said.

"I'll look it up," she said sounding dubious. Then she shook her head. "But then I can't get back to you." She made a wry face. "You forgot your phone again."

"We can discuss it at the next class," he suggested. "On Monday."

"I have to miss on Monday," she said.

"Friday, then," he said.

Her expression was as dubious as her voice had been. At least she didn't say no.

⌒

The following week followed in the footsteps of the previous one. He got a message on his landline from the doctor's office with instructions on how to sync his fitness device with the doctor's computer system. There was a user name and a password and some other stuff that he ignored. He was supposed to call and tell them when he'd done that.

Otherwise, the week was unexceptional.

Until Friday.

Friday morning had a sparkle to it. Not that mornings didn't normally sparkle, but he found this one made him feel especially alive. The light and the smell of the damp ground, rich with earth smells released by an overnight rainstorm, blended together to give it a strange zest.

But things that start right can go wrong, and when Lyle stopped to gas up his car, he found a sign on the pumps saying: "Temporarily offline."

Inside, he found the bored clerk reading a book. "What does it mean... offline?"

"They are doing system updates," the clerk said.

"On gas?"

He nodded. "On the pumps, but yeah."

"I can't get gas?"

"Not until the updates finish."

"When is that?"

"When it reboots."

With no idea what that meant, Lyle postponed his purchase.

At work, he learned that the boss was thinking of investing in some new machine tools.

"They'll increase productivity and accuracy of the machining," she said.

"Will you send us to a class in how to run them?" he asked.

"The computer runs them," she said.

He thought of the gas station being offline. "What about when it's offline?" he asked.

She scowled. "We call tech support. But the machines can run twenty-four/seven, unlike human operators."

That raised an obvious question. Knowing he wouldn't like the ominous answer, Lyle didn't ask it, but he knew he'd gained a small appreciation for Ned Ludd and his view of the world.

On this particular Friday, the bank seemed crowded. He got in line and waited, knowing he would see Becky and be able to bask in her sweet, uncomprehending smile.

An unusually large man stood just inside the doorway, his hands folded in front of him. He seemed to be watching. He was dressed in jeans and a blue denim work shirt... nothing special. Periodically, he glanced in the direction of the front door. He seemed to be expecting someone.

Moments later, two other men came in through the door. They wore long coats, and as they entered the lobby, they opened them, pulling out shotguns. One man had two under his coat. As he passed the big man, he handed one to him. The big man turned and locked the front door.

When he turned back, all three men had their weapons pointed at the people milling about the lobby. Lyle's heart pounded and his mouth went dry. He'd never had a gun pointed at him before in his entire life. He could honestly say now that he knew he didn't like it. Not at all.

"This is a robbery," a second man said in case anyone hadn't figured it out yet. The three men spread out, covering the entire lobby. The big man shouted: "Everyone on the floor," and he moved toward the tellers.

Lyle's world change gears. People did as they were told in slow motion. Around him, unreal figures put up their hands and sank awkwardly to the ground.

The big man put a hand on the countertop that separated customers from tellers and vaulted over it, effortlessly, it seemed. The panicked tellers were dropping to the ground and the man looked enormous, silhouetted by the later afternoon sun pouring in through the large window that looked out at the drive-through on the far side.

The situation was so odd, so unreal, that he didn't even notice he too had put up his hands and dropped to his knees until he saw one of the bank robbers looking down at him.

"Face down on the ground," the man said, his voice a menacing growl.

Lyle lay down. Getting into an altercation with men like these was not on his to-do list. Of the many things that needed doing, that was not one.

The large man had set about the task of collecting what cash was in the tellers' drawers. Lyle couldn't see Becky. She had to be on the ground behind the counter where the robber was.

A second man began walking around the lobby, holding out a bag. "Put your phone, your wallet, and your watch in the bag," he said. Each person dutifully did as he or she was told, then the robber moved on, repeating the phrase as he moved from one person to the next. The third man stood watch covering the room from the door.

The people universally showed intelligence that surprised Lyle--they did exactly what the robbers demanded.

When the man got to Lyle, he got up on his elbows, removed his watch, and put it in the bag. Then he slopped his wallet from his pocket and did the same.

"Phone," the man demanded.

"I don't have one," Lyle told him.

"What do you mean?"

"I don't have a phone."

"Everyone has a phone."

"Not me."

"I want your phone."

"I'd give it to you if I had one."

"This guy says he doesn't have a phone," the man told the big man, who had returned from his exploration behind the counter carrying a large bag.

The big man came over and kicked Lyle in the ribs. He gasped as the stab of pain shot through him. "Give up your damn phone," he said.

Lyle had his hands near his face. He hated that he was trembling. "I don't have one. I've never had one."

"That's crazy," the big man said. Putting down the bag, he grabbed Lyle by his collar and yanked him to his feet, tearing his shirt. "Pat him down."

The other man frisked him, searching for the phone that just had to be there. "Nothing," he said. "Maybe he left it in his car."

"Is that where it is?" the big man asked.

"I don't have one anywhere," Lyle told him.

His head jerked to the side and pain shot up his neck. It took a moment, which he spent falling to the ground, to work out that he'd been hit.

"Stop screwing around," the big man said. "Cough up the damn phone or I'll start breaking your bones."

"We don't have time for this," the man by the door said. "Forget his phone. We don't need it."

"There is a good reason he won't give it up," the big man said. "What's on it, buster? You got a digital wallet, don't you? I bet you've got a bundle in cryptocurrency on it and lousy password protection."

"I don't know what you are talking about," Lyle said. His brain raced, looking for scenarios that didn't end with these men killing him. He should have said it was in his car, but it was too late now. Besides, they might just drag him outside and make him get it out of the car.

"That's it." The big man was triumphant.

"The cops are going to get here soon," the man by the door said. "You know some fool set off a silent alarm."

"I'm not getting trapped in some stupid hostage situation for some crypto that might not even be there."

"I'm telling you…" the big man said. "The guy doesn't carry the phone around because he knows we could crack it."

The sound of a siren in the distance caught his ear.

The man by the door made a face. "Damn it, I'm out of here." He turned and unlocked the door and looked at the other man. "You coming?"

They both looked at the big man. He finally snorted and the three of them dashed out, carrying their loot.

No one in the bank moved. Moving required knowing where it was safe to go.

"That was so brave," a woman near Lyle said. "I couldn't have done that."

"Wasn't it?" a man asked.

Suddenly, they were all getting up and patting Lyle on the back.

He watched them. His jaw ached and he was sure he'd broken a rib. Maybe two, and yet, oddly, he felt great. When he saw Becky smiling over at him, he felt even better.

"I saw you on the news," Irene said. "You are quite the hero."

"I didn't really do anything."

"You refused to give up your phone. That's what the news said. And because you kept those men in the bank, the police were able to grab them in the parking lot as they tried to leave. No one was seriously hurt." She touched the yellow bruise on his jaw tenderly. "All those people said you were incredibly brave."

"They are being generous."

"What about that French restaurant?" she asked.

"You want to go?"

"I looked it up online and it sounds great." She smiled. "How about tomorrow night? I can make reservations and text you the details."

"I'd love that," he said.

He looked at her face. "I have to admit something," he said. "I have a new phone and have no idea how to use it. Could you help me?"

Her face lit up. "I'd love to. We can get you on a chat."

"If you say so," he said. "It seems a lot different than any phone I've had before."

"Oh, they are always changing them so much, sometimes it's like starting from scratch."

"Exactly," he said. "You'll need to treat me like someone who has never used a cell phone."

She laughed, delighted. "That would be weird, someone who'd never even used one."

"I'll bring it Saturday," he said.

"Fantastic."

On his way home he noticed a phone store near his house. He'd get one in the morning.

As he pulled into his parking spot at his apartment he wondered if there were any other Luddites around still, or if they'd all surrendered, as he was about to. The idea of being the last Luddite on the planet was as intriguing and bizarre as being the inadvertent hero of a bank robbery.

He'd staved off the intrusive technology for years. Now that he was giving up, the moment had a bittersweet quality to it: bitter from giving in; sweet because Irene would be teaching him how to live in her world. He'd lose whatever he had and gain companionship.

And there was a secret bonus. If he was ever robbed again, he'd have a phone to give them. Broken ribs were painful.

THE END

ABOUT THE AUTHORS

J. Lee Porter is a former IT specialist, programmer, and data analyst for banking, security, and government agencies. He left the IT world behind on July 4, 2016, declaring it his personal Independence Day to travel the world full time in search of inspiration for his writing.

Jeff is on Twitter at @JLPorterAuthor
His website is www.nomadicgiant.com

Ed Teja is a writer, poet, musician, and boat bum. He writes about the places he knows and the people who live in the margins of the world. After being friends with tech giants, pirates, fishermen, and a coterie of strange people for many years, he finds the world an amazing place filled with intriguing, if sometimes crazed, characters.

You can contact Ed on Twitter at @ETeja
His website is www.edteja.com

If you liked this story, please leave a review.

www.ingramcontent.com/pod-product-compliance
Lightning Source LLC
Chambersburg PA
CBHW071231130626
46555CB00004B/1943